FORTY DAYS

40 NIGHTS

by

MYRON BISHOP

Dorrance Publishing Co
585 Alpha Drive
Suite 103
Pittsburgh, PA 15238
Visit our website at *www.dorrancebookstore.com*

ISBN: 978-1-6376-4357-0
ESIBN: 978-1-6376-4669-4

FOREWORD

Myron Bishop has a very good imagination! If you didn't already know that, you will by the time you read these pages.

Myron has chosen to ask the "What if?" question about the forty day period between the crucifixion of Jesus of Nazereth as described in the Four Gospels and the ascension of Jesus to heaven described at the end of Mark's and Luke's Gospels, and at the beginning of the Book of Acts, which continues the story of the work of Jesus' followers over the next few decades.

This approach to what might have taken place during the mysterious forty days and nights is interesting, creative, and a very entertaining and thought-provoking read. As Myron told me in conversation prior to sending me the manuscript, this is not intended to be a book of theology. But that doesn't keep it from being one of the most interesting takes on the "forty days and nights" between Jesus' crucifixion and ascension I've ever read.

The way we handle the mysteries and gaps in the Bible's narratives could benefit from more people with imagination asking the "What if?" questions! I hope that you have the "imaginational bandwidth" to enjoy Myron's approach to Forty Days and Forty Nights as much as I did!

Jim Stephens
Pastor, Missionary, Author

This book is dedicated to our friend Dennis K. Hartley who is singing in God's choir.

Peter asked Jesus why we are we going to Golgatha? Jesus answered even as we approach death we are reminded that eternal life is just beyond. Peter asked where have you been lately. Our members almost forgot what you were teaching. Jesus told Peter I will not be here, in the flesh, to remind the flock of the teachings. Jesus said that is why I have chosen these men to carry on my teachings. Jesus said my word is for the world, not just a chosen few.

When they approached Golgatha a Roman Centurian approached Jesus. Peter started to step up but Jesus waved him off. The Centurian looked into Jesus' eyes and said I have been waiting for your return. Jesus asked what could he do for the Centurian? The Centurian said I am one of the soldiers who lifted your cross up to the upright position. The Centurian said I found that your tomb was empty and I have been here every day waiting for your return. Jesus said I have a job for you if you are willing to leave your employment in the Roman Legion. The Centurian said I am at your direction. Jesus said follow me, Tiberious. The Centurian knew that Jesus would not have to ask his name, his belief was now absolute.

Jesus approached his disciples and introduced Tiberious to them and told Peter this is the person I have chosen to carry out my instructions to you. Peter acknowleged that he would carry out the instructions Jesus had given him.

This group that Jesus had chosen to accompany him now included, Mother Mary, Mary Magdalene, Peter and the rest of the disciples. Tiberious hung to the back of the group, not sure where he fit in.

When they reached the crest of the hill Jesus turned to,the group and said, verily I say unto you believe in me and you will not fear death because eternal life awaits you. Jesus said I must return to my Father but at a later time I shall return and claim my flock. From here you are to go forth and teach the word.

The dark clouds parted and the sun shown through bright and clear. As the group watched Jesus floated in the air and was raised up into the heavens.

The group was still in awe at what they had witnessed. They sat around, in the house, and discussed what had Just happened. At least they were all in agreement that this was a special event in their lives. Jesus had allowed them to see who he really was.

Peter worked his way over to Mary Magdalene and said I need to ask you some questions. I need to know where Jesus and you disappeared to in the last forty days. Mary Magdalene said I can tell you the whole story, but it needs to be told in its entirety and will take some time. Peter said we have time to listen before we scatter to the world to preach the word of Jesus. The attention of everyone was now placed on Mary Magdalene.

Mary Magdalene started with Jesus asked me to go with him on a mission. I didn't ask him where we were going I just agreed to go.

Mary Magdalene said I went to sleep at the night and when I woke up Jesus wasn't in the house. I stepped through the door to the outside and was met with a rainy climate of green grass, shrubs and trees. I was cold to my bones and shivered. A lady placed a cloth around my shoulders and said something in a language I couldn't understand. Jesus spotted me, smiled and said good morning and immediately I could understand the language the people were speaking.

Jesus was speaking to a group of children and they were laughing and playing. An Elder walked up to Jesus and asked him where he came from. I was fearful for Jesus' life at that moment, but as Jesus spoke the Elder smiled and my fear was lifted. Jesus walked up to a child that was sitting on the grass by himself because he was blind. Jesus reached out and touched the childs face and said see me. The child opened his eyes and jumped up and hugged Jesus and ran after the other children saying I can see. The Elder was impressed and asked Jesus if he could heal the sick? Jesus said all things, in my father, the only God, are possible. Soon people were bringing the lame, sick and dying to Jesus. Jesus made no exceptions on who he would heal.

Jesus had the Elder walk with him to the top of the hill. Jesus stopped and placed a rock on the ground and he walked 40 paces away and placed another rock on the ground. Jesus walked 40 paces in a direct square and placed another rock on the ground. Jesus then walked 40 paces to make this a square. Jesus said build me a church here and whenever you are here I will be also. The Elder asked Jesus if he understood where he was. Jesus said with a smile I always know where I am. We are in Britannia and we are at Roslyn.

That is the first time I knew where we were at said Mary Magdalene. Jesus had the ability to take us anywhere he wanted to go.

We stayed in Britannia for a few more days so Jesus could preach and heal the people. While we were there they started the foundation to the church and promised Jesus that it would be finished, no matter what.

I went to sleep at night, with joy in my heart, knowing that Jesus was doing what he was meant to do and no church leaders or Romans would stop him.

I woke up on a special morning waiting for what would happen next. I stepped out of the house that I had been sleeping in into a total different world. I was in a forest of trees by an ocean bay. Jesus was waiting for me and said we have work to do. We walked into a native village with houses built of tree limbs, leaves and mud. Jesus addressed the first person he met, yet again in another language. As they were talking small children came up to me. The children hugged me and held me close. I was amazed at how the children were innocent of fear of someone different. Jesus and I were led to a house occupied by the leader of the village. He had been sick for some time, even though he was younger than me. The village was waiting for him to die and a replacement had alrady been picked to sucede him. Jesus took the sick man's hand in his and said, quietly, arise and follow me to your future. The young leader stood up and walked out of his house into the light of his village. Jesus said you need this leader to take you into the future.

We stayed two days so Jesus could spread his word and heal the sick. Jesus told the leader your future depends on your ability to satisfy the needs of your people. Jesus said prepare yourself for the coming winter as it will be colder than usual and your enemies will want the comfort you build up.

Mary Magdalene said I had asked Jesus where we were at and he informed me, we were in the new world and that it would remain unspoiled from greed and coruption for a millinia. I asked Jesus if he could stop the changes. Jesus told me only man can change.

Some of the surrounding villages had heard of the great healer and they were now bringing their sick to Jesus to be healed. Jesus always found a way to preach a sermon of respect and love to the new people arriving daily. Mary Magdalene said I enjoyed our stay in this village because of the respect they put in the women and elders. No where had I been treat-ed like this before. I was hoping we could stay here a long time but Jesus told me our time was short. We had many stops to make before it was over. At that time I did not understand that we had actual time restraints on us.

I was amazed at the animals and birds around us. The birds were so large they had a difficulty flying. The people could walk among the birds and they wouldn't fly away. The people would pick out a bird and hit it with a club and drag it away while the other birds just watched. Some animals looked like our donkeys but were larger. The animals had horns but they were crooked with many points. The people could walk almost all the way up to them and then would shoot them with bow and arrow. The rest of the animals would not run. It was strange but the large animals had skin that was strong and the people made their houses and clothes out of it. Plus the meat was very good when cooked over a fire. I haven't really got the words to describe everything I saw.

Jesus never told me when we would move on. I would just wake up in the morning and walk out to a new surrounding.

I walked out of the hut in the morning and Jesus was standing beside a large muddy river. Jesus held out his hand and said walk with me. I was nervous and I know Jesus could feel it. Jesus said your trust in me will be justified. Jesus stepped out onto the river, with me in tow. It seems like we were walking on a cushion of air. The river was very wide, wider than our Jordan. We arrived on the other side of the river after a long time. Jesus smiled and said the new village is just over the hill.

We walked over the hill and down into the village that was beside a small river. When we walked into the village the only people that were there were the elders and the children. Jesus asked where the rest of the people were? We were told that the village was out on the hunt. The herd was migrating by and this was the time of the year that the village could fill their supply of meat for the coming winter. As if on cue a dog with a sled attached approached the village with the sled piled high with hides. The dog and sled were led by a young girl, probably not more than 10 years old. As soon as the sled was stopped in the village the elders and children started unloading the sled onto the ground. As soon as the sled was unloaded the young girl turned the dog around and headed out of the village. Jesus asked if he could go with the girl. The girl shrugged and didn't say anything.

Jesus followed the young girl out of the village and over a small rise. As soon as they got over the top of the rise the hunt came into view. Jesus could see that everyone was working to clean the meat. Off to one side of the butchering area 3 people were standing over a pile of skins. Jesus walked to them and asked if he could see what they were protecting. The 3 people pulled the skins off the body of a young man. One person spoke up and said that this person had beem trampled by the herd. Jesus leaned over the body, touched his head and said Running Wolf wake up, you are needed by your people. Running Wolf opened his eyes and stood up. Running Wolf hugged Jesus and walked back to where the work was. The people who had been standing over Running Wolf were just staring in amazement. When Running Wolf approached the rest of the people they just looked on in amazement. Some of the people had to touch him to make sure it was really him. The chief of the tribe came up to Jesus and asked if he was the great spirit? Jesus said I am the Son of the only one true God and I am here to help people. The chief said we have some wounded from the hunt and asked can you help them? Jesus said I can assist anyone in need.

Mary Magdalene was amazed at the size of the hides that were being piled up. She asked if the beast were really that big? One of the elders said that the herd stretched to the horizon and could take a complete day to pass. Most of the animals stood as tall as the tallest man in the village. The elder said the earth would shake when the animals were on the run. Mary Magdalene asked what were they going to do with the hides. An elder told her some of the hides would be scraped of the hair and tanned to make clothes and tepees. Other hides would be made into robes and blankets with the hair left on. Most of the meat would be dried for use when the winter snows came. Tonight the village would feast on fresh meat.

All the meat had been loaded on sleds and was being taken to the village. Jesus walked with the Chief back to the village. The Chief asked Jesus how long would he be gracing their village with his presense? Jesus said I have only so much time to give and so many places to go, but I will stay with your people as long as I am able to help. The Chief said that is all we can ask for. The Chief asked Jesus what do I tell the people who you are? Jesus said I am the son of the one and only true God and I am here to spread his word. My hope is that you will carry on this tradition in some form. Jesus said years ago God gave a rightous man his ten commandments to live by. I will give these to your people.

When they entered the village Jesus could see the fires and structures made ready to dry the meat. As soon as the sleds stopped they were being unloaded and the meat being prepared for drying. This day would be hectic and Jesus knew he would have to stay out of the way and only do what he was asked. Not long into the process a young lady was brought to Jesus with a deep gash on her arm. She was bleeding profusely and needed immediate attention. Jesus touched her arm and immediately the bleeding stopped and her arm was healed. Nobody said anything nor were they amazed at the healing. The word had been passed on how Jesus had saved Running Wolf.

It was late in the evening when most of the work was done and the meat was hanging over the fires to dry. Now all that was left was to make sure the fires were kept burning. Meat had been cooked in clay pots for the evening meal. Jesus was asked if their was anything special he needed to say. Jesus said let us say a prayer for our meal. Jesus lifted his head to the sky and said, Father thank you for this bounty that will sustain our bodies. The chief looked at Jesus, smiled and looked at the sky and said, great spirit we thank you for your care and for your sacrifice of these beast to sustain our existence in your world. The chief offered Jesus the first bowl of food. Jesus smiled and said I would like my companion, Mary Magdalene, to be the first to partake of this food.

The very next day tribes from all over the area started arriving in the village. The word of the healer had spread rapidly on the prairre. Jesus was given a place of honor in which to speak to the tribes. Jesus preached his message of love and honor to the rapidly growing group of people. He stressed that the worship of God was a way of salvation.

When the sermon was over the sick, lame and injured were brought before Jesus. Jesus was not one to turn anyone away when they were in need.

Jesus had just healed a person suffering from boils when a middle aged native came forward and accused Jesus of being a fake. He said that Jesus was using magic to appear to heal the sick. Jesus didn't say anything he just reached out his hand to grab the hands of the accuser. Whithin seconds the man screamed and jerked back. The man's hands were bleeding in the same place that Jesus had been hammered to the cross. The man fell to his knees and said I saw you get nailed to a cross but you are still here. Jesus said I am here to do my Father's work until he takes me home. The man said you have to be the one true man of God. Jesus said spread your belief amongst your people.

Mary Magdalene went to where the woman were preparing the hides for tanning. Mary asked if she could be of help. One of the woman showed Mary how to scrape the fat off of the hide in preparation for tanning. As Mary watched one of the women squatted and urinated on a hide. Mary flushed with embarassment and the woman just laughed. She said this is the way we have always worked the leather. Mary said I will help you scrape the fat but the rest you will have to do. The work was tedious but rewarding and Mary enjoyed learning new things.

That night Jesus came to Mary Magdalene and said soon we will be moving to somewhere else. Jesus said I have finished my ministry here.

When Mary Magdalene woke up the next morning she was expecting to walk out to a new area. Mary was not expecting what she saw. Mary was in an area of tall mountains with smoke coming out of the peaks. This was very unsettling to Mary as she had never seen any thing coming close to this in her life. Jesus told Mary they call this the land of the big smokes. These mountains are still young and forming. The people expect that these mountains can erupt at any time. Jesus took Mary Magdalene by the hand and they walked into the village. The village was in a state of frantic activity. Jesus asked what was happening from the first person he met? Jesus was told they were preparing to cross the river and go upstream to the falls. The fish were migrating up river and this was the time to prepare for the coming winter. Jesus asked where was the chief at? The person he is at the head of the caravan. Jesus thanked the man and then walked to the beginning.

As Jesus approached the head of the caravan the Chief looked up and said I think you are looking for me. Jesus said we are here to join your people for a short time. The Chief said you are welcome here, but remember we have a job to do. Jesus said we will wrend assistance where we can. As the neared the river the Chief said we are going to cross on the bridge of the Gods. Jesus said I presume that is the land bridge accross the river. The Chief said it is what our tribe has been using for ages. Jesus told the chief that the bridge was only temporary and would crash into the river in years to come. The chief said I see that you are a seer. Jesus said my Father lets me see into the future on certain things. The Chief asked

Jesus if his Father was one of the Gods. Jesus said my Father is the only one God. The chief said we believe in many Gods. Jesus said that is why I am here to teach you that there is only one true God.

The ground was shaking as they crossed the river and the people were getting nervous. Jesus said it is not yet time for the bridge to go into the river.

The tribe turned and headed up the river after crossing the bridge. The Chief told Jesus it would take them more time to get to the falls so they would be camping for the night at the rapids.

The ground around the rapids was hard scrabble and the vegetation was sparse. Even with this hardship the people were in good spirits. Jesus took this time to preach of the only one true God. Jesus answered any questions that were asked. One woman brought her Mother up to Jesus and said she had been blinded by age. She said if Jesus was who he said he was then he should be able to cure her Mother. Jesus said I am the truth and the light. Jesus looked into the face of the Mother and could see she was blinded by growing cataracts. Jesus touched the eyelids of the woman and said God has invested in letting you see again. The Mother opened her eyes a cried out I can see. That statement alone brought more people to see Jesus. As people gathered around Jesus he took the time to heal the sick and the weak. Jesus brought forth the teachings of the original 10 commandments. One of the people said we are a peaceful and non-waring tribe. We try to respect the rights of all the people around us. Jesus said wars should only be used to protect your family, not domination.

Mary Magdalene went with the women to look for berries. As they walked along the bushes Mary asked what she was looking for. One of the women pointed out the types of berries that were edible. Mary was told that tonights dinner would be sparse but by this time tomorrow they would be eating fish. One of the women called out she had found a porcupine. Mary had never seen this type of animal before and hung back while someone killed the animal. Mary asked why the animal had to be killed? The person who had found the porcupine said we use all of this animal. The quills are used to weave patterns for clothes. We dye the quills to colors we want, after we cut off most of the tips. The meat will be put in a pot and cooked with local vegetables. The insides will be left for the birds to eat. As if on cue the woman showed Mary the beautiful design that had been made and placed on her moccasins. Mary was amazed at this and told them she was impressed.

They arrived at the falls in the afternoon of the next day. The Elders went to the "Long house" for a planning strategy for all of the tribes present. Every tribe would be assigned a certain area to fish. This system had worked for years without conflict. Jesus was impressed on how all of this had been worked. Jesus asked how long before the actual fishing would start? Jesus was told the tribes would first offer up prayers for the safe return of the fish and for the safety of all who would be participating. The actual fishing would start the next morning at dawn.

Jesus walked to the river and looked over the falls. He could see the scafolding that they would be fishing from. Jesus understood the risk that this would take. Jesus watched as a fish jumped up into the falls and fell back down. Jesus could see that the journey would be dangerous for both the fish and the people.

The morning came, bright and clear with dew on the ground. The women had been up earlier starting the camp fires and fixing breakfast. Now the men were rising from their sleep and preparing for the day. This was a somber occasion and some faced it with fear in their heart. The river, at the falls, was ferocious and unforgiving for anyone making a mistake and falling in.

Jesus watched as the men stepped out onto the scaffolding and used long handled nets to dip in the water. Jesus was amazed that the men could hold onto the net after capturing a fish. These fish were the size of a small boy and were equally as hard to hold on to. Every time a fish was in the net the person capturing the fish had to walk back to the bank, of the river, and give the fish to the women to take care of. This process was repeated over and over. There seemed to be no lack of fish.

Jesus watched in horror as a man fell from the scafolding and fell into the water. A cry went up that a man had fell into the river. Jesus didn't hesitate he just walked out onto the river and ducked under the water. Within a few seconds Jesus pulled the man from under the water and took him to the bank of the river. Jesus placed the man on his side and pushed on his back. The man started coughing and spewing water out of his mouth. Jesus stepped back and gave the man room to breath. Soon the man stood up, looked at Jesus and went back to the scafolding. Before he stepped out on the scafolding the man turned to Jesus and said God is with me because of you.

Mary Magdalene was helping the women prepare the fish. They taught Mary the art of scraping the scales from the fish and how to carefully remove the insides. When fish roe was found it was to be put in a clay pot filled with water. Mary was told that when a sperm sack was found it would be emptied into some of the buckets also. Those buckets would be taken up-stream and into other rivers and dumped into the water. This method was used to hopefully preserve fish for the future. This is what had been done for years and was not questioned. As Mary cut into the fish Mary could see that the flesh was firm and a red-dish orange. Some of the women were biting off some of the flesh and eating it raw. Mary had been taught to never eat raw flesh so she ignored the taunts from the other women to try the raw fish. Mary was just as adept as the women around her and had no problem keeping up.

It was a long day and no other incidents of people fall-ing into the river, to a great relief of the people. As the people sat around the fires at night, eating fresh cooked fish, some of them drifted over to where Jesus was sitting. The accepted the miracle, as they were calling it, as a fact belonging only to Jesus. Jesus took this time to preach about his Father being the one and only true God. When Jesus was asked if he could heal the sick his response always was bring them to me and my Father will allow me to heal them.

Through the early evening hour Jesus was kept very busy healing different ailments. Always Jesus gave the praise to his Father as the one and only true God. The people seemed to accept his version of events and Jesus had no reason to doubt their word.

The Next morning 4 young men were preparing to go up river with the clay pots of fresh fertilized fish eggs. Jesus asked if it was alright for him to go with them? Jesus was curious as to the method being used. One of the young men said we will be moving fast as we have to go to 2 different rivers and then go up stream. Jesus said I have no problem keeping up. Each young man picked up 2 covered pots and started off on a run.

It wasn't very far to the first river and 2 young men turned up river. Jesus had to decide which men to follow and decided to keep going up river to the fartherest point. The terrain at the first river looked rough and Jesus hoped the second river would be easier, even though Jesus didn't get fatiqued. It was turning to dusk when they approached the second river. The young men set up a cold camp at the mouth of the river. Jesus talked to the young men about what they were doing. One of the men said our ancestors have been putting these fish eggs back into the river for years and we carry on the tradition. Jesus asked do you know if these eggs ever produce a new run of fish? A young man said tomorrow you will see the return of the adult fish that have escaped from the falls. He said I think you will be impressed.

At the break of dawn the young men picked up the clay pots and headed up the river. As they reached one of the first pools of quiet water Jesus could see that the number of fish stretched almost completely accross the river. One man said we have to go further up river to a quieter spot. After crawling over rocks and onther impediments they came to a quiet pool just below some fast running water. At this point 2 of the clay pots were emptied into the river. Just a short juant up river they came to another quiet spot and the last 2 pots were emptied into the river. Jesus asked what happens when the other fish get up to here? One of the young men spoke up and said they will see this is occupied and continue further up river. One of the men said we have stayed here before and watched the outcome.

Upon trekking back down the river they found that the canoe they had left to cross the first river, from the falls was missing. On the other side of the river the first 2 men were waiting. The said that when they had got to the mouth of the river the canoe was gone. they presumed that it had gotten loose and floated down river. The water was running fast and would be a danger to try and swim accross. Jesus said grab my hand and follow me. The 2 young men looked at Jesus questionally and then reached out for his hand. Jesus stepped out onto the river and with the 2 men in hand walked accross the river. When they got to the other side of the river the 4 young men said you are truly a God. Jesus said I am the Son of the one and only true God. Jesus said go and preach what I have told you to the native dwellers of this country. All the way back to camp Jesus answered questions and preached on the way of salvation. Jesus reminded these young men of the 10 commandments that were given to man years ago.

Back in camp there was a line of people waiting for Jesus to heal them. Jesus didn't disappoint any one and helped every one who was waiting for him. Jesus preached his message of love and forgiveness.

Jesus approached Mary Magdalene and told her that she needed to take the time to say good bye to all of the friends she had made because tomorrow they would be in a different area. Mary knew to not question what Jesus was saying and said this time will be difficult for me as I have made many friends.

As light shown into where Mary had been sleeping, Jesus stood in the doorway and said to Mary, please be careful when you step out. Mary walked to the door and looked out, and down. They were high on the side of a cliff. Jesus said we are with the cliff dwellers in a semi-arid area. These people have forged a lifestyle of safety. They are mostly farmers and do little foraging for animals. Mary looked out at the view and thought it was amazing. Mary looked down to where the women were working the fields. Jesus just smiled and said be careful stepping down the ladder.

An Elder approached Jesus and said we have been waiting for you. Our ancestors have passed down the information that you would come to us some day. A smile from Jesus said it all. The Elder said, to Jesus, follow me. Jesus turned and told Mary that he would be busy this morning and for her to enjoy the clear bright day.

Jesus followed the Elder to the communal house. The leaders of the tribe were waiting for him. As Jesus entered all the members stood up. Jesus said I am here for you. One of the people said let me see your hands. We have been told that you would have the marks of the cross. Jesus held out his hands for all to see. Jesus said your legends are accurate. The Elder motioned for Jesus to take the seat reserved for only honored guest. Jesus said the end of the world is not yet ready to come. Jesus said I am here to answer any questions you may have. One of the people asked is the time of the end near? Jesus said only my Father knows. This seemed to satisfy the questioner. A man, with a crooked leg stood up and asked if he was the great healer? Jesus said walk to me. As the man stepped forward his leg straightened up and his limp was gone. Jesus said, does that answer your question.

Jesus took the time to preach his message of redemption and peace. Jesus said I will heal the afflicted when they are brought before me.

A man broke into the meeting with a gesture of regret He stated we are being attacked and the women are in danger. Jesus abruptly stood up and walked out of the house. As Jesus approached the cliff he could see many men approaching the women. An elderly woman was ferociously trying to hold off the attackers to let the rest of the women escape. Jesus watched as the woman was stabbed.

Jesus jumped from the cliff and floated down to the ground while the attackers looked on. Jesus reached the woman, who had been stabbed, first. As Jesus reached down the woman's stab wound closed and she was healed. Jesus turned his attention to the attackers and said this has to stop right now. One of the attackers unleashed an arrow at Jesus and Jesus stopped the arrow in the air and directed it into the ground. Jesus said to the men, lay down your weapons and we can talk. The attackers were stunned and realized that this was not a mortal man. Without any hesitation the weapons were all laid down and the men bowed their heads in reverence to Jesus.

Jesus said I don't know what grievances you have with these people but it is time to talk rationally to each other. By this time the Elders had descended to the ground and were standing behind Jesus. Jesus said no weapons are needed. Let us all sit together and find a common ground to become friends. Jesus said I am here to heal the sick and deformed. I will not tolerate any animosity in my presence. There was nothing but silence. Jesus asked the cliff dwellers, first, what was the problem. The leader said we have always been enemies. They attack us and we retaliate. Jesus said my Father has given you only so much time on this earth and you need to make the most of it. This does not include making war with each other. Jesus told the attackers to go and bring their sick to him. Jesus also said spread the word to other tribes that I will be here for a short time and they are welcome to come and here my message of peace. I will take the time to talk to all of you. The leader of the attackers asked Jesus if he would make sure they were safe when they came here. Jesus said no man will lift a finger to harm you in my presence.

Mary was awakened by Jesus standing in the doorway. Jesus said, to Mary, today will be very busy. The tribes have started to gathe for guidance and truth. Jesus said I will need your help today. Mary said but I am just a mortal. Jesus said you have more power than you think. Today is a day that will go down in folklore for the tribes to pass down for generations. Without any more words Jesus descended to the area where the tribes were waiting for him.

For Jesus seeing the tribes sitting together, in peace, was the beginning, hopefully, of them learning to live together.

The line of sick and deformed limbs of the people was very long and exhausting. After a few hours Jesus ask-ed the cliff dwellers to bring him a basket of bread and a basket of dried meat. With only a small basket, of each, the Elder asked how could we even begin to feed all of these people? Jesus didn't say anything to the Elder, instead he said a prayer. Jesus said Father bless the people for being here in peace and let them know that this food is nourishment for their human bodies. With the prayer said Jesus instructed that the food be passed out. As the baskets were carried to the people eager hands grabbed for the food. After the first group of people were fed and the baskets carried to more people they were astonished that the baskets were never empty. A murmer erupted into a loud clamor as more people got food. The people understood that only a man of God could accomplish this feat. Jesus finished his healing and preaching with a retelling of the original 10 commanments.

As Jesus stood in the doorway he told Mary the site you see today will be beyond anything you have seen before. Mary stepped out of the house and was greeted by a bright sun. In amazement Mary looked at the pyramid that stood in the center of the town. Something like this could only be explained in a dream. The pyramid had 91 steps on each of its 4 sides. The top of the pyramid had an alter. Jesus told Mary that this was a monstrousity that was used for the wrong purpose. As Jesus was talking to Mary a priest approached with a young girl in tow. Jesus stopped the priest, who was dressed in bright feathers and a painted face, and asked him what the girl had done wrong? The priest said this is a young virgin to be sacrificed to our God. Jesus said God does not ask that young virgins be killed in his honor. Jesus unbound the girl and told her to go home and live a normal life. The priest got angry at Jesus and told him he had no right to change what they had been doing for years. Jesus had a hard time controlling his anger at this priest but told him that his father would not agree with him and this form of sacrifice had to end. The priest told Jesus that another virgin would be picked for the sacrifice. Jesus was so wrought that he lifted his hand to the sky. The ground shook and the pyramid tumbled into small stones and created a hill. The people cowed at this and lay prostate on the ground in reverence to Jesus. The priest said this is blasphemely. Jesus said this is God's will. The priest reached for a spear to throw at Jesus. As the priest lifted his hand, with the spear, Jesus pointed at him and said begone from my sight. The priest vanished in front of the people.

Mary had never seen this side of Jesus and was afraid for the people and she said so. Jesus told Mary that the priest had been sent to stand before God but he would be returned to the people.

Mary looked around in amazement to where she was at. A large lake lay directly in front of her. Almost as large as the salty sea she had occasion to see at home. She was surrounded with mountains higher and larger than almost any she had seen before except for the mountains of smoke. The area they were at was being farmed. There was large plots of ground that were planted in what the local people called maize. Also visable were large gourds and pumpkins. Mary had never seen this food at where she was raised but this resembled the food the cliff people were farming. Apparently, in their history, the 2 people had met and given each other the secret to growing this food for their use.

The people were short in stature coming up to Mary's shoulders. Their complexion was darker than Mary's, but not as dark as the people she had seen from Africa. Their features were almost perfect in looks, with most of them featuring tatoos over a large part of their bodies. Piercings in the ears was done on most of the women. The hair of the men was cut very short and the women's hair were braided. This was unusual because it was uniform for all of the people.

The people carefully approached Jesus not being sure of how to react to him. Jesus said come to me and sit at my feet. I will tell you the story of redemption in God's sight. Jesus opened his telling with I am the Son of the one and only true God. He has sent me to you to enlighten you on the true path to heaven. A man spoke up and asked how do we know you are the true path? Jesus looked at the man, and as he did a glow surrounded Jesus and a dove descended to Jesus' shoulder. A gasp went up among the people. Just as remarkable the Priest, that Jesus had sent to God, reappeared in front of Jesus. Jesus asked the Priest if he had repented his sins? The Priest prostated himself in front of Jesus and said God almighty had seen fit to give him a second chance in life. The Priest said I am here to serve you. Jesus asked the Priest what God had told him? The priest said God gave me 2 choices. He opened up the bows of the earth and showed me what living in hell would look like, both past and future. I got to see the effects of the bad deeds some people had created. God let me understand that I was the only one who had a choice in what path I took. Jesus said I think that you have chosen the path of enlightenment and truth. The Priest said I am going to follow the one true God and preach the word he has given me.

Jesus turned to the people and said I am going to be here only a short time. The Priest will carry on my work after I have departed from you. God has given these commandments to live by. Jesus related the ten rules of God's commandments and asked the Priest to take the time to memorize them. Jesus said it was up to the Priest to try and get his people to live a righteous life.

Jesus turned to Mary Magdalene and said walk with me to the lake. Mary wondered what was going to happen next. As they approached the lake Jesus said to Mary I needed a little time to understand what the future holds for these people. Jesus told Mary that within 2 generations these people would forget what they were being taught. Mary asked why was Jesus preaching these commandments? Jesus said I want to save as many people as I can. This will stop the sacrifices of the innocent for years to come. Mary ask-ed if something couldn't be done permanently? Jesus said human nature eventually will take over and greed will lead the way. Mary asked Jesus if he would come back to these people in their time of need? Jesus said only my Father knows when I will be allowed to return. Jesus said you are the only person who knows how hard this is for me. Jesus told Mary I have chosen you to walk with me on this path so that you can relate to the trials that are to come. Mary said I have seen both the good and bad in the people we have visited. Jesus said we have more people to visit. Tomorrow we will be in a different place with a different type of people. Jesus said you must understand I will not let anything bad happen to you on your journey. I have a special place for you.

Jesus took Mary back to the waiting people. Jesus said bring your sick and infirmed to me. Jesus spent time healing people with the Priest in attendance at all time. Jesus told the Priest my Father will let you heal the sick if your faith is strong enough. The Priest said I am only God's vassal and he will dictate what I will be allowed to do. Jesus said that is all I can ask for.

As Mary stepped through the door to the outside the humidity hit her with a force she had not felt in her lifetime. She stepped through the door into a world of tall trees blowing in the wind. Mary looked behind her and could see an expanse of crystal clear blue water that extended beyond the horizon. Mary was awestruck with the view. Mary looked at the people, who were staring at her and Jesus, and noticed that most of them were plump and had a shine to their skin. The women were wearing a grass skirt and no top. This was astonishing to Mary that these people understood life and did not seem to lust at each other. One of the women approached Mary and put her hands on her as if to find out if she was real. Mary just stood there and let the woman touch her. Then strangely the woman hugged Mary and said welcome to our Island. Mary was stunned but managed to say thank you. The woman took Mary's hand to lead her to where a group of people were sitting on grass and talking to each other. Mary looked at Jesus and he smiled and said go with the lady and enjoy yourself. You have earned it.

Mary was introduced to the group, Mary did not know how the woman knew her name. Mary had to assume that Jesus had planted her name in the lady's mind. Mary looked over the food that was offered. She had not seen most of the fruits and vegetables. Mary was given an object that was round and hard and had holes, where one hole had been punched out. Mary was told to drink. Mary, cautously, took a sip. The liquid was very tasty and Mary drank more. The people seemed to relish the idea of a newcomer, they called her a Wahine. Mary was given a yellow fleshed fruit and it was sweet and juicy. Mary looked at the rest of the food and couldn't understand how they could be plump on this food. The fish was well cooked and seasoned with the juice of a green fruit. Mary was enjoying the food and told the group so. The group said wait untell this evening. We are having a Luau in your honor.

Jesus walked to the water where the men were getting ready to go out fishing. The boats were different from any he had seen before. The boats were long and narrow and had outriggers on one side, one in front and one in back. One of the men told Jesus my boat has room for one more if you want to come with me. Jesus stepped into the boat, carefully so not to rock it from side to side. The man pushed the boat out into the water and jumped in. With Jesus this boat had 5 men, 2 in front of Jesus and 2 behind him. All 4 men paddled the boat out onto the open water. They sang while they were paddleing.

When they were out far enough, where they could still see the land, they stopped and set the net. This part of fishing Jesus was familar with. Within minutes the net started to sink into the water. The men immediately pulled the net to the boat. The net was heavy with fish. Rather than unload the net into the boat the men anchored the net firmly to the side of the boat and rowed to shore. Jesus had a quizical look on his face and one of the men said this keeps the fish fresh until we get to the shore and we don't need more than one netfull at a time. The man explained the weather was so warm that the fish would rot in a day so they only net what they needed each day. When they got to the shore Jesus helped unload the net onto the grass. The men were careful to throw back into the water the types of water animals they weren't going to eat. Jesus enjoyed his outing onto the water but now it was time to get back to why he was here. Jesus told the people he was here to spread the word of God and to heal the sick. The king stepped forward and said we have been waiting for you. Jesus was astonished that he was expected. The king explained our Fathers told us of a person coming to us with a message of hope and forgiveness. We were told he would heal our sick. Jesus said let me prove to you I am the one you have waited for. The king waved his hand and a wman was carried forward on a stretcher. Jesus asked if anyone knew what had happened to this woman? The king said she fell ill and into a coma and has been like this for a full cycle of the moon. Jesus asked did she eat something that might have been poisonous? The King said we don't know for sure. Jesus reached down and touched the woman's stomach. Jesus closed his eyes and prayed, Father please release this woman from the grip of the poison. The woman shook, opened her eyes and said I am hungry. The people clapped and bowed. They said welcome back king's mother. Jesus understood the meaning of this healing. Now others were coming forward. The lepers were the last to come to Jesus and the people made a clear path as they were declared unclean.

That night, at the luau, Jesus preached his mesage of

the one and only true God with compassion for others. Jesus repeated the ten commandments and told the people to keep them in memory. The king asked Jesus to sit with him. Jesus accepted and as they sat beside each other the king asked Jesus how long he would stay with his people. Jesus answered I won't be here long. I have to visit other people before my time on earth is up. Jesus asked the king why he didn't question Jesus' valdity before? The king said I saw the holes in your hands and that was part of the lore. The king said our forefathers were very specific on what we needed to look for.

Jesus came to Mary at the end of the Luau. He told her to be prepared for tomorrow we will be in another land. Mary never questioned Jesus because she knew what he said would be true.

Peter stopped Mary at this point saying we are getting tired and need to rest. We can pick up your story on the morrow. Peter turned to the disciples and said get some rest. Tomorrow we will hear more of the story. Not a disciple complained as it had been a long day. Peter turned to Mary Magdalene and said I need to ask you a personal question. Peter asked Mary were you and Jesus intimate? Mary was shocked at this question. Mary assured Peter that Jesus had not initiated any personal contact. Peter said I didn't think so but needed to ask the question. Mary said I thought you knew Jesus well enough that he was not interested in that type of relationship, plus he is too busy with his mission. Mary said I will give you Jesus' response when I finish the tale of his travels.

In the morning the disciples were in a hurry to get the chores done so they could get back to Mary relating the story of her travels with Jesus.

As Mary walked out of the door she was greeted with a sight of a green paradise of a pool surrounded by flowers and trees. The background was of a tall mountain with a whisp of smoke coming out of the top. Mary turned and looked at the houses and they seemed to be flimsy put together. The entry doors were very thin with small squares of almost opaque paper and slid to open. Mary stared at the women. The women were dressed in long flowing dresses that tied in the back. The womens faces were painted with a substance akin to flour and the eyebrows were painted dark brown with their lips painted ruby red. Jesus told Mary they are called Geishas. They are here to serve the men. Jesus said they are not prostitutes. Jesus said they shower the men with the affection the men desire. Jesus said they serve the food and drink. Give massages and even bathe the men.

Before Jesus could give Mary any more information a strangely dressed man with a long sword rushed at them. Jesus pointed his hand at the man and he was gone. Jesus said don't worry I have sent him back 3 days in the past. He well not bother us again. Mary was used to Jesus' powers and did not question how he did things.

Jesus told Mary follow me. As they stepped through the gate to the city outside they were met with a scene of people hurrying to do their normal day. Even though they were dressed differently Jesus and Mary drew no extra attention except for a glance here and there. Jesus said these people are used to having strangers in their midst. Jesus and Mary had just stepped out of the Warlords housing complex.

Jesus stopped one of the men and asked where was temple? The man turned to Jesus and said you need to turn around and go away. Jesus smiled and said he was not worried for their safety. The man then shrugged and gave Jesus the directions he needed. The man told Jesus that there would be guards at the entrance and that they turned away everyone. Jesus asked why do you have a temple you can't use. The man said they extract a tithe from every one who lives here. The man said the priest rarely come out of the temple to see the people. But when they do it is usually for a public execution. Jesus asked if the people were going to see a public execution? The man said it is mandatory for all to come and see. Jesus asked what was today's execution for? The man said someone approached the center of the temple without permission. The man said he was debuking the priest for their way of life and for their actions to the people. Jesus' thoughts immediatley went to his cousin John. Mary knew what was going to happen next as she followed Jesus and the people to the temple.

When they approached the temple Jesus pushed his way through the people to the front where the execution was being held.

A man, in ragged clothes, was on his knees at the entrance to the temple. The man was defiant in the knowledge of his impending doom. A priest, in white flowing robes, was standing next to the young man. Beside the man was a person dressed in warrior clothes with a large sword held above his head. Jesus approached the priest and said this will not happen. As Jesus stood in front of the priest the sword disappeared from the warriors hand. The people gasped and the warrior dropped to his knees in supplicant to Jesus. Jesus turned to the man and his ties to his hands and feet disolved into dust. Jesus turned to the priest and said you have been abusing your power over the people for your personal gain. Jesus said this will stop now. Jesus pointed at the gates to the temple and they disappeared. Jesus said the temple will now be open to all the people. The priest said the head priest will not allow this. Jesus said you will find that your leader has disappeared into the gates of hell. With that statement the priest disappeared from in front of the people. Jesus said from now on this temple will be dedicated to the one and only true God. As Jesus spoke the people knelt down to him and to his power. Jesus said stand up I am only the messenger here to deliver the message of God.

As Jesus sat on the steps to the temple a young boy, probably 3 or 4 years old, crawled up on Jesus' lap. The boy looked up at Jesus and said Master tell me my future. Jesus looked into the eyes of the boy and saw a gentle man of the future. Jesus said, to the boy, you are destined to become a leader. Jesus said, to the boy, Your words and deeds will be remembered long after your body has passed into history. With that being said the young boy reached up, patted Jesus on the cheek and jumped down and ran away.

Jesus said I am here to heal the sick and to preach the word of the one true God. Jesus said the original 10 commandments, given to the people, will be left with you. As if by magic a scroll appeared beside Jesus with writing on it. Jesus said these should be kept in the temple and open to the people to read. Jesus said I expect the new priest of the temple to teach the people to read.

A woman came up to Jesus and said my son is at home and is dying. The woman said he is too sick to come to you. Jesus told the woman to go home and cook a meal for her son. Jesus said he will greet you at the door. The woman looked at Jesus with skeptical eyes and Jesus said you came here for a miracle. It is time for you to believe.

Mary decided that she needed to go back to the house that they had come to this land. Mary had more questions for the ladies that were there. Mary approached the house with trepidation. She knew she may not like the answers she would get, but she knew she would ask them anyway.

The women surrounded Mary Magdalene, like she was an honored guest. Mary was led into a house and instructed to sit, on her knees, in front of a table. Mary found a bowl of steaming rice was served on the table in front of her. As Mary picked up the chop sticks a young girl giggled. An older lady showed Mary how she was supposed to use them. Mary was very deft and the learning process was very fast. Now a bowl of steaming soup was produced in front of Mary. A spoon was not evident so Mary looked at the older woman, as if to ask how do I eat this. The older woman said you pick it up and drink it like you would any onther liquid. Now that was done a bowl of meat was produced in front of Mary Mary did not ask what kind of meat because she didn't want to know. Finally a sticky cake was served with a small glass of a clear liquid. Mary turned to the oldest looking lady and asked her what happens when you get to old to serve? The lady said normally we have found a household to move into to take care of a family until the end of our lives. The lady said sometimes a young servant will find a handsome man who wants to marry a virgin. The lady said all servants here are virgins. Having sex in this house is forbidden. Mary asked how did you come to be in this house? The lady's answer was simple. My family was very poor and they sold me to this house when I was 5 years old. The lady said I have lived here ever since. The lady said we all have been trained in the fine art of taking care of men.

Mary realized it was getting dark and she was very tired. This day had been very eventful. Mary said I am very tired would you please take me to where I will be sleeping. The lady nodded and a young girl, not more than 10 years old, told Mary to follow her.

Mary entered a room that was bare of any decorations except for a sleeping mat on the floor with a roll that was to serve as a pillow. Mary was so tired that she was asleep as soon as her head hit the pillow.

Mary stepped out of the room and into a large open square. Mary could see a large ornate building with steps leading up and into the building. Mary was staring, in amazement, when 2 guards rushed at her. The guards stopped at what seemed to be an imaginary wall not far from Mary. Jesus appeared beside Mary and said follow me. We are in the Emperor's courtyard and no woman is allowed to be here without permission.

Jesus and Mary stepped through a gate and out onto a very busy street. People were rushing, mostly in one direction, to a destination for whatever purpose. Mary asked where is every one going in such a hurry? An old man said we are at the Emperors discretion as a work force to build a wall. Mary asked how big was the wall? The old man answered only the bosses know for sure. Mary was amazed that Jesus had not uttered a word during this exchange, and she said so. Jesus answered you were doing good without me.

As they neared the wall they approached a courtyard and a man knelt in the middle, with people huddled around. Jesus could see a warrior standing over the man with a sword raised in the air ready to chop off the man's head. As the arm started to come down the sword disappeared out of the warrior's hands. Jesus said only God has the right to take a life. Jesus asked what has this man done? As Jesus spoke a man appeared from behind the warrior. The man said I am the boss and what I say goes. Jesus asked again what has this man done? The boss said he refused orders to climb the tower. Jesus turned to the man and asked did you do what they claim? The man said 5 people have already fell to their death climbing the tower. They have no safety precautions in place. Jesus asked if this was true? The boss said we are building a wall with guard towers. We don't have the time to do extra work for protection. Jesus said I think it would be of benefit to you to provide safety. The boss said men are cheap and we have an endless supply. Jesus said the people deserve better. The boss started ranting at Jesus and his voice went mute. Jesus said I have heard enough of your ranting. It is time a rational man came foreward and answered for the emperor. As Jesus was speaking he hadn't noticed that the people were on their knees in supplicant to him. Finally a man came out of a building on the edge of the wall and asked if he could clear up the problem? Jesus said I think some of your bosses don't take in consideration for the wellbeing of the people. The man said the bosses can become over bearing as they are working on a commission basis of what they get done each day. Jesus asked what has made life so cheap that it is acceptable for men to be lost on the job? The man said we have come to accept the fact that some lives will be lost. Jesus said I expected a better answer. The man, noticing what was happen-ing around him, asked what can I do to have your permission to proceed with the project? Jesus ans-wered you need to listen to the plight of the people and ask them for their help, and ideas in making your project safer. The man said the project is shut down for today. We will start fresh tomorrow. In the mean-time the people need to select a person to come to me with their ideas on safety. I promise whomever comes forward will not suffer any persecution. Jesus turned to the people and said please stand up. After the people stood up Jesus said you have an opportun-ity to shape your own future. The man, who had al-most been executed, spoke up and said are you the one who is to deliver us from this persecution? Jesus said you are the only ones who can do that. I am here to do God's work and preach his commandments to the people. Jesus said I came to here heal the sick and injured.

Mary remembered a temple they had seen on their way to the wall and decided to go back to it and see what was inside. As Mary entered the temple she saw a large statue of a fat bald man gilded in gold. Mary asked, one of the robed priest, who this man was? The priest said the statued depicted the man who had given the people wise sayings. Mary asked if he promised a way to get to heaven? The priest said his sayings were only about how to live life on earth. Mary said then he didn't promise salvation. Mary told the priest you need to take the time to go and talk to Jesus. The priest asked if that was the man at the wall? Mary said Jesus is the Son of the one and only true God, through him you get to heaven.

As Mary and the priest were talking a man burst into the room and said Jesus was healing the sick and lame at the wall. The priest said no man alive has the ability to do that. Mary butted in and said Jesus had been crucified and risen from the dead. Mary said Jesus is not a mortal man. The priest ran out of the room, with the man, and to the wall. The priest ran up to Jesus and said what right do you have to heal the sick.

Jesus said I need no permission from you to do God's work. The priest was humbled in Jesus' presence.

Mary fell asleep on the floor, next to the statue. The hubub of men talking finally roused Mary from her slumber. Jesus and the priest were discussing divinity. Jesus was explaining his right to declare who he was. Finally Jesus looked at the statue and said he looks so grim. Jesus said from this day on any statue, of this man, will have a smile. With that statement the statue, and all like statues, had their facial expressions changed to glee. Jesus said this is just a statue of a man. God has demanded that no statues of him be made. Jesus told the priest you are doing good works, but they will not allow you into heaven. You must believe in the will of God. The priest prostated himself in front of Jesus and said I believe in God in heaven.

Jesus turned to Mary Magdalene and said, it is time for us to go. When they stepped through the gate to the outside Mary's breath was taken away by the chill and the altitude made it hard to breath. Mary asked Jesus where are we? Jesus said we are high in the mountains to seek the reason for the people's belief in a mortal man. Mary said I am chilled and do need some form of clothing to help me. Instead of clothing Mary Jesus entered a storefront and obtained a heavy sherpa jacket. Mary was grateful for this show for her well being. Jesus said it is time we went to the local temple.

On entering the temple they observed a very young boy sitting on the throne. Jesus went up to the boy, and a guard stepped forward. Jesus held up his hand and the guard receded into the background. Jesus asked the boy why he was here? A priest stepped forward and said he is the new leader of our faith. Jesus asked again, to the boy, why was he here? The boy responded they came to my house and took me away from my parents and installed me here. Jesus asked by what right do these people do this? A priest stepped forward and said when our leader died we were directed to a house to find our new leader. Jesus asked who directed you to take a young boy away from his parents? The priest said we just followed our way through the village until we found the house of a family with this young innocent. Jesus said the key word here is innocent. Jesus asked the boy if he wanted to go home? The young boy had tears in his eyes when he said I have been told this is my home from now on. Jesus said no religion has the right to subjegate anyone beyond their personal will. Jesus reached out to the young boy and said follow me I will take you home to your parents. The young boy looked over at the priest as if asking permission to leave. Jesus said they will not hinder your return home. To the priest Jesus said to find a leader you must look to a man of an age old enough to make a decision. Someone among your followers must have the atributes you seek.

Jesus took the young boy to his birth home. Jesus walked up to the door and knocked, expecting an answer. When no one answered Jesus tried the latch and found the door locked. Jesus had no problem to open the door. Jesus walked into the room to find a man and woman huddled in the corner. Jesus asked the woman if she was willing to welcome her son back home? The man spoke up and said he is no longer our son. Jesus said I asked the woman, not you. The woman said my son was given with the understanding that he would be the next leader. Jesus asked who made the decision to give up your Son? The woman said the man of the house makes all decisions. Jesus asked, truthfully is this man the Father of your Son?

The woman said the father died from an accidental fall from a cliff. Jesus said when you marry a woman you accept her family as yours.

Jesus went to the cemetary and told Mary Magdalene to wait at the entrance. Jesus walked up to the grave of the dead Father and said I want to talk to you. As people watched from afar a figure emerged to talk to Jesus. Jesus asked how did you die? The man said I slipped and fell from the cliff. Jesus said turn around so I can see all of you. When the man turned around Jesus saw 2 hand prints on the man's shoulders. Jesus asked who was with you at the cliff? The man said I was accompanied by my best friend. Jesus asked if his best friend was connected to the local religion? The man said his Father is the head priest. Jesus said sleep will my friend I will take care of your Son.

Jesus was surrounded by people when he left the cemetary. They were all talking at once trying to get answers to what they had just witnessed. Jesus told them to be patient. Everything would be clear soon enough.

When Jesus returned to the house he found the head

priest waiting for him. The head priest said you need to leave things alone. Jesus said your Son pushed his friend off the cliff to marry his girl friend. Your Son did not know the girl was pregnant at the time. You helped your Son cover up the murder and as soon as the Son was old enough to take to the church the leader mysteriously died and the child was removed to the church. Jesus said I think you are complicant in both murders. The people gasped. Jesus said things like this have been happening for centuries. Jesus said I think the 2 of them should be bound over for a trial and justice be done.

A citizen of the village approached Jesus and asked if he would be the judge for the trial? The man said that usually the religious leader would be the judge but his demise made that impossible. Jesus said I will sit and listen but the final decision will be my Father's.

The decision was made to try the Son first and then the priest. Jesus asked the man tell the people what happened on the day your friend died? The man said my friend was standing at the edge of the cliff and his feet slipped. He said I reached out to stop him from falling but I couldn't grab him. Jesus said what if the evidence may say something different. The man said their is no other evidence. Jesus didn't say anything but looked beside the man and then the man killed appeared beside him. Jesus asked can you see your hand prints on his back? Jesus said they are pushing not grabbing. The man was shocked at the evidence standing beside him. Finally flustered he stated I did-not know the girl was pregnant with his child. She is the most beautiful girl in the village and a common-er shouldn't have the right to have her. Jesus said that still doesn't give you the right to kill him to get the girl. The man said you and your people are hyp-ocrits. David killed his friend to obtain his wife. Jesus said that still does not justify what you did. Jesus said I see no remorse in your actions, only excuses. Jesus said I find you guilty as charged and you will be sentenced to join your friend, except your grave will be unmarked to let you rest in obscurity. With those words both men vanished from the court room. Jesus then asked the priest to come foreword and sit in the witness chair. Jesus said the head priest died under mysterously circumstances. Jesus asked what do you have to say? The priest said the leader was old and sick. I just helped him into the after life. Now Jesus was irritated and it showed. Jesus said this does not give you the right to assist someone to death. The priest said he was going to expose my Son. What did you expect me to do. Jesus said your Son's crimes were his own. You should have let him stand trial on his own merits. The priest said I did what I thought was best for the young boy and our religion. The young boy was never going to be liked by his step-father. The boy was a perfect candidate to be groom-ed to be the next leader. Jesus said this still does not give you the right to manipulate the situation. Jesus said my sentence is to strip you of all your worldly goods and banish you from this village and country for all of your mortal life. In your wanderings you will have the opportunity to redeem yourself. Make good use of your opportunity. Jesus said justice has been done.

Jesus took the rest of the day to heal the sick and to preach the message of God. At the end of the day he told Mary Magdalene tomorrow they would be in a new place. Mary said I am glad we are moving on. I don't like the cold or how hard it is to breathe at this altitude.

When Mary stepped through the door all she saw was

sand and scrub bushes. Mary was at the confluence of 2 rivers. She asked Jesus what were they doing here? Jesus answered hold my hand as we step forward.

Mary grabbed Jesus' hand and they stepped forward into the desert. On the seventh step the desert disappeared and they were in a beautiful garden like Mary had never seen before. The perfume aroma from the flowers was estatic. The trees had flowers that gave out the beauty of the area. The stream was surrounded with grass and green bushes. Mary could see fish swimming in the water. Mary remarked on the beautiful colors and smell that she was feeling. Jesus said if you live here why would you want to go to any other place? Jesus said follow me I want to show you something.

In the middle of the garden was a tree that was dried up, misshapen and ugly. Jesus said this is the tree of forbidden fruit. Jesus said once it was green and vibrant. Then when it was violated it turned into this. Mary said do I dare ask who violated the trust of the tree. Jesus said you have heard the story all of your life. Now you are seeing the actual ending to that story. Jesus said I wanted you to see what was before the betrayal.

Jesus told Mary to walk in the garden and enjoy the beauty because before long they would be leaving to return to the world.

Jesus left Mary alone to enjoy the beauty surrounding her. Jesus stepped to the tree of life and said Father I need to ask a question. Jesus asked his question and was told of the eventual outcome of his question.

Jesus walked up to Mary and said have you enjoyed your surroundings? Mary said I could live here the rest of my life. Jesus said I wish it was possible for you, but for now you will have to wait out your normal life span before you can come here again.

Jesus took Mary by the hand they walked out of the garden and back into the desert.

Jesus said we have to go into the city. Jesus said I have to talk to the religious leaders and hope for an understanding.

As they neared the city Mary could see the beautiful hanging gardens and she remarked to Jesus that if the people were as beautiful as the outside walls why would they need to change. Jesus said people put on a front to look beautiful, just like these walls. Inside people are truly themselves. Jesus said these people worship false Gods and statues.

When Jesus and Mary entered the city Jesus went to the temple to talk to the leaders. Jesus was stopped at the entrance and told to take off his shoes Jesus remarked I am not wearing shoes. Jesus said I am here to tell you about the one and only true God. The priest said we have many Gods. Jesus said your worship of these false Gods well undermine your ability to seek justice and right. The priest asked have you seen our beautiful city? Jesus said the outside walls are beautiful, but the inside city is dirty and grim. Jesus said I am the truth and the light. Jesus said my Father has sent me to you to give you the word. The priest said You will have to prove who you are. Jesus looked at one of the statues of a God and it fell into a pile of dust. Jesus said my Father has said you shall not have false Gods before me. Jesus said you are not to worship idols. Mary was not shocked at the outcome.

She had seen Jesus transform to be more assertive in what he wanted. The priest said any good magician can make a man's mind see what he wants it to see but the statue still is in its original form. Jesus said walk up to the statue and touch it, then tell me it is still standing. The priest walked up to the statue and touched the sand it had become. Jesus asked do you see what I see? The priest said you destroyed a statue of Baal. Jesus said if you look around you I have dest-royed all the false Gods statues. The priest asked what am I supposed to tell the people? Jesus said you are to tell them there is only one true God and no statues of him are to exist.

Jesus told the priest that in a near time he will send a prophet to them to preach the truth. The prophet will come from Mecca. Jesus said the prophet will be a breath of fresh air preaching peace, love and forgive-ness. The prophets teachings will be written down for future generations. Jesus said be weary that some will try to twist his teachings into a call for submission and war. Jesus said the prophet will not preach war. You must listen to the true words of the prophet.

Jesus said I am here to heal the sick and spread the

word. Jesus said bring the people to me that need to be healed. The priest sent a runner into the crowds to spread the word of Jesus' presence.

The first person to approach Jesus was a blind beggar. Jesus asked the man how long he had been blind. The man said he had been born blind and his parents had abandoned him when he became too much trouble to take care of. Jesus asked do you believe in miracles? The man said I have been waiting my whole life for a miracle. Jesus touched the man's eyes and said open your eyes to a new world. When the man opened his eyes he saw the world around him and kissed Jesus' feet. The man said master I am yours to command. Jesus said go forth and spread the word that there is only one true God. Jesus added God will be with you.

A woman came up to Jesus and asked if he could raise the dead? Jesus said my job is not to correct the time of life cycle. If it is time for a person to go and be with God I will not change it. The woman said my husband did not have an opportunity to meet you. Jesus said if your husband was a rightous man he will walk with God. The woman was satisfied with this explanation and walked away.

The crowd parted as a lepper came forword. The murmer of unclean went through the crowd. Jesus reached out to the lepper and the disease left the man's body. The former lepper reached out to Jesus and said I am yours forever. Jesus said you are to preach the truth forever. The lepper asked if he could bring the rest of the lepper colony to him? Jesus said return to your colony and your presence will heal all who are sick with the disease. As the lepper departed the crowd reached out to touch him.

Just as Jesus had figured the priest of the false Gods was trying to turn the crowd against him. Jesus said anyone who speaks disparging of the true God will have their tongues silenced forever. A murmer went up from the crowd as the priest's tongues went silent. Jesus said the one and only true God is the one you are to heed his words. I have sent a healed blind man to you to teach the way to salvation.

Jesus took Mary with him as he walked the city and healed anyone who came to him and asked for his help. Jesus told Mary that adoration was fleeting and that they would soon foreget him. Mary said she thought his legacy would live on. Jesus said probably in some form but the actual allusion would fade from memory. Jesus told Mary to enjoy the city and people today because tomorrow they will be in a different place.

Jesus was waiting for Mary as she walked out of the door. Mary could hear laughter of children playing in the distance. The weather was warm and the sun was brighter here to Mary. Jesus told Mary they were in a place where Adam and Eve had fled to when they were ejected from the garden. Jesus said because their survival skills were limited this was the best place for them. The weather was mostly warm, even at night. There are caves in this area where they could seek safety. The plants and trees are rife with fruits just for the picking. Adam and Eve had not learned how to kill yet. Mary asked how can these people be part of our past, their skin is darker than ours? Jesus said time and climate has changed the skin color but they are still the same people. Jesus said as Adam and Eve's children scattered around the world the characature of their skin was changed. This explanation was good enough for Mary.

Jesus said they have erected a temple to hold the

bones of what they believe are the first people to live here. Mary asked Jesus if these were the real bones of Adam and Eve? Jesus said it really doesn't make any difference. They believe it is what counts. Mary asked if they would be allowed into the temple? Jesus said yes, except we won't be allowed near the ossuary where the bones are kept, that is their holy of holies.

As Jesus and Mary entered the temple they were approached by an Elder and told to remove their shoes. Mary did as she was told and Jesus showed the Elder he wasn't wearing shoes. As the Elder inspected them he noticed the scars in Jesus' hands and feet. The Elder said you are the holy one we have been expecting. The Elder said it is written that you would come into our world to visit us and heal the sick. Jesus said I am the one, bring your sick and believers to me. The Elder said I have sent a runner to tell the people you are among us.

Jesus asked if they could see the room where they keep the ossuary? The Elder said only men are allowed in the room where the ossuary is kept. The Elder said you will be allowed into the room but we will not open the ossuary. Jesus said that is ok I do not desire to touch the sacred bones.

As Jesus entered the room he was greeted by the head priest. The priest bowed in reverence to Jesus. Jesus said that he was grateful for the reverence. The priest said it is written, in our history, that you would come to walk among us for a short time. The priest said that it is written that you will wash away our sins. Jesus said I am here at the direction of my Father, in heaven, who made this world. Jesus said man has been the one to destroy the tranquility and peace in this world. The priest said this has also been passed down in our history. The priest said we are the place man, and woman, fled to after the first great sin.

When Jesus exited the holy of holies room Mary had already left the temple and was among the children. The children were laughing and telling Mary stories of the great migration that had brought their ancestors to this area. The children explained how this had become the cradle of civilization. Mary was amazed at how much the children knew. The Elder told Mary that children are easy to teach, for good and bad. Mary asked if the children were being taught bad? The Elder said we try to teach only the reality of where and how we live. The Elder said we want our children to grow up with the knowledge of the past.

As Jesus approached Mary and the children, a child with a club foot came up to Jesus. Jesus reached down to the child and the club foot was healed. An act of kindness was met with a smile and a hug from the child. The children then encircled Jesus and all of them reached to Jesus to admire him. Jesus held out his hands, to the children, to show the scars and to let them know he was here for them, also.

The head priest approached Jesus and said Master I have assembled the sick and weary for you. Jesus said lead me to them. As Jesus followed the priest Mary and the children came with them.

Jesus walked into the crowd of waiting people, healing as he went. Jesus let everyone know that he was the Son of the one and only true God. The religion of the people was the teaching of the story of the creation. Jesus was thankful that the true religion was being taught to the people.

When the day was over Jesus told Mary our trip is almost done. Tomorrow we will be back in Judea and I will be going home to be with my Father. Mary asked if she was to go with Jesus. Jesus said you will remain on this earth for the rest of your days. The only thing that will change is that you will live the rest of your days outside of Judea. Jesus said I have addressed the concern for your safety. I will send a centurian to watch over you.

Mary's story to the disciples was complete. Peter said it is time for the disciples to spread the word. As they dispersed Peter could hear some of the disciples grumbling about why Mary was chosen to accompany Jesus and not one of them. Peter ignored the comments as he knew that the questions would be answered in due time.

After the rest of the disciples had left Mary told Peter I have one more thing to tell you and Jesus told me I was only to tell you. Peter said I am listening. Mary said on the last night Jesus touched my belly, with his hand, and said that I would carry his lineage forword. Peter asked, did he give you a reason? Mary said only that this line would be kept secret from the rest of the church. Mary said Jesus asked his Father to allow this to happen. Mary said Jesus knew the church would not want to hear this and the secret should be kept until well into the future. Peter said I understand this is why Tiberious is to accompany you to another place. Tiberious will be your protector for the rest of your life.

Early the next morning Tiberious told Peter that he and Mary would be leaving that day. Tiberious told Peter that he had been given 40 pieces of silver for the trip. Tiberious said I don't know how far that will take us, but I will make sure we get to where we are going. Peter asked do you know where you are going? The answer from Tiberious was that he would be showed the way as they went. Tiberious said he trusted the lord, Jesus, to give them the guidance. All Peter could say was have a safe trip.

As Mary and Tiberious left the house Tiberious told Mary they were going to Joppa, on the coast, to see if they could get transportation, by sea, to Rome. Mary asked if Tiberious would have any problem walking in public. Tiberious said I have discarded my Roman centurian outfit so I will just be a regular person out for a walk. Mary asked if the Roman army would come looking for him? Tiberious said I think Jesus has taken care that so that Rome won't be looking for me.

The trail to Joppa wasn't the most defined and finished and the struggle to navigate the trail wasn't very easy. Tiberious could see that Mary was getting tired so he made the decision to stop at Beth-horon for the night. Finding lodging wasn't easy as the people were wary of strangers. After visiting the market place and asking questions Tiberious finally found a place for the 2 of them to stay and have some food to eat. The cost for the 2 of them was 2 pieces of silver. This was probably double the normal cost because of who they were. Tiberious didn't complain he just paid and they were led to their room. The room was almost completely bare. A mat in the corner with something woven to resemble a blanket on top of it. Tiberious was told food would be ready in 30 minutes and the morning meal would commence at 0700. Tiberious said that would be fine and asked where they could clean up. Their host led Tiberious and Mary to a courtyard with a pond of water and a sheltered place, not to far away to relieve themselves.

By the time Mary and Tiberious had cleaned up it was time for the evening meal. During the meal their host kept questioning Tiberious about events around the area. Their host was most interested in the rumors coming out of Jeruselam and of the crucifixion of the one called Jesus. Tiberious didn't want to get into the conversation but Mary spoke up and said that Jesus had kept his promise and rose from the dead in 3 days. Their host asked where was this Jesus now. Mary said he has gone to live with his Father in heaven. This was all that was said and this seemed satisfy their host and no more questions were forthcoming.

Back in the room Tiberious explained he would sleep at the foot of the bed and Mary would have the rest of the bed. Mary was so exhausted that she fell asleep immediately. Tiberious lay awake thinking about how their fate was intertwined with the intentions of Jesus.

Tiberious felt Mary stirring awake and was immediately up. Mary said the first thing on the agenda this morning is to relieve myself and clean up. Tiberious had already became accustomed to Mary saying exactly what she wanted and meant. Tiberious led Mary to the courtyard and watched over her while she entered the small shelter to relieve herself. After Mary came out to to the pond Tiberious went into the shelter and relieved himself. Tiberious came out to the pond and took his time to make sure he was clean.

Mary and Tiberious entered the house just as the meal was being placed on the table. This morning there was very little small talk as their host seemed to have something else on his mind. The host said we have packed a small lunch for you to take with you. Their host said it can be a long way between places to find food. Tiberious was wondering if their host was trying to find out which direction they were going. Tiberious just said thank you for your hospitatlity and Mary and he departed. Tiberious told Mary I think we should never tell any of our hosts where we are going. Mary agreed and asked if she shouldn't have volunteer-ed any information about Jesus? Tiberious said I think our host already had been told almost everything you told him. Mary smiled and said I am not used to being in a position to have information for people.

The end of the day brought them to the port city of Joppa. Lodging here was easier to find and Tiberious had secured lodging very quickly. The room was more spacious and had 2 beds. The price was less than they had to pay in Beth-horon.

After getting something to eat and settling Mary in the room Tiberious told Mary he was going to go and get them passage on a ship to Rome. Tiberious told Mary to stay in the room. Tiberious said Joppa could be dangerous for a single woman out in the city.

Tiberious approached the ship yard with the idea of who he would try to get passage for the both of them. The idea was to try to get as safe of passage he could find. Tiberious approached a Phoenician ship and ask-ed if he could come aboard? After boarding the ship Tiberious asked to see the Captain. Tiberious was led to the Captains cabin and the sailor knocked on the door. After a couple of seconds they heard some scurrying around and a closet door closing. Then a gruff voice said enter. The sailor smiled at Tiberious and opened the door to the cabin.

A very husky tall man was sitting behind desk in the corner of the room. The Captain was a little flushed and Tiberious knew better than to ask why. Tiberious said I need to secure passage for 2 people to Rome.

The Captain asked how come he didn't contact a ship with Roman registry? The Captain said he knew one was in the harbor. Tiberious said that may be true but I know that no one dares attack a Phoenician ship.

The Captain asked Tiberious if he had served in the Roman military? The Captain also asked if Tiberious was running from or hiding from the military? The Captain said he only needed to know if he would be hiding a fugitive so he would know how to react if he was confronted. Tiberious said I used to be a Cent-urian but now I am a private citizen and nobody is looking for me. The Captain asked the sex of the other passenger? Tiberious said she is a female but would pose no problem for this trip. The Captain said the price would 10 pieces of silver for each of them, paid in advance. The Captain said we are going to sail at first light and if you are not here we will leave with-out you and your money will be forfeit. Tiberious ask-ed if he could see the accomodations? The Captain asked if he needed special consideration for the trip? Tiberious said That he just prefered the accomoda-tions be on the upper deck. The Captain said I see that you have been on the open sea before. Tiberious said below deck can be treacherous and as time goes by tends to get a little smelly. The Captain smiled and told the sailor to take Tiberious to the cabin they would be assigned to. The Captain asked if he needed their food to be delivered to the cabin? Tiberious sad that would be prefered. The Captain said that would be 5 more pieces of silver. Tiberious handed the Captain 25 pieces of silver for the trip and left the cabin with the sailor.

Tiberious was shown a cabin mid-ship. Before they entered the sailor marked the center of the door with a red X. The sailor turned to Tiberious and said that was to let the men know this cabin was off limits. Tiberious asked if that wouldn't draw attention to the cabin? The sailor said all of the men have sailed with this Captain before and are aware of the rules and what would happen if they broke the rules. Entering the cabin held a surprise for Tiberious. It had more of a luxerious feel than he had expected. The sailor explained that passenger accomodations were better than shipmates. The sailor said we do get requests to take on passengers quite frequently. The requests are because people know we offer safe passage. The sailor explained how to lock the door, from the inside. Tiberious asked what about locking the door from the outside. The sailor said the Captain prefers that the passengers refrain from walking about the ship. The sailor said everybody aboard ship knows not to enter any cabin unless permission is granted. Tiberious asked if any new hands were added in this port? The sailor said our crew stays the same and if we need to add anybody we wait until home port. Tiberious just shook his head and thanked the sailor and left the ship.

Tiberious woke Mary just as soon as he saw that dawn was breaking. Tiberious told Mary that the ship would be sailing at dawn. Tiberious said we need to hurry to the ship I have already paid for our passage. Mary asked what they were going to do for food? Tiberious said I have arranged for our meals to be delivered to our cabin. This satisfied Mary and she gathered her things.

Upon entering the cabin Mary was surprised at how well it was furnished. Mary said maybe this trip won't be too bad. Mary said I do want to be on deck when we depart. This well be the last time I see my homeland. Tiberious said the Captain prefers we do not mingle with the crew. Mary said that might be hard to do on a trip of this length. Tiberious said we should be in Rome in 7 to 10 days, depending on the weather.

As they pulled out of port Mary got to see her homeland for the last time. Instead of a tear, like Tiberious expected, Mary was smiling as they were leaving. Mary said the only good thing to happen to me, in my homeland, was Jesus and he is no longer here. Now Tiberious could understand the smile.

Soon after they entered their cabin Tiberiuos heard a knock on the door. When he opened the door a lady was standing there with a tray of food. Tiberious took the tray and said thank you. The lady said I will be back in one hour to pick up the tray. The tray consisted of meats, cheese and orange juice. Tiberious was pleased with the selection. This trip may not be as bad as he had suspected.

After the sun had gone down for the day Mary asked Tiberious if they could make a walk around the deck to get some fresh air? Tiberious said I am not sure that the Captain would approve. Mary said we can't stay inside this cabin for the complete trip. Tiberious said let me check the deck to see if it is safe.

Tiberious made a trip around the deck and came back and told Mary to cover her head, she needed to reduce her chances of being recognzed. Mary did as she was told and they left the cabin. Tiberious placed a small peg against the bottom of the door. He wasn't taking any chances on anyone entering their cabin.

One time around the deck for Mary was enough. The ship was rocking in the waves and this made Mary nervous. Tiberious asked Mary if the rocking was making her sick? Mary said no, but I have never been out on the water before.

They had just entered their cabin when a knock came on the door. Tiberious answered the door and the lady from this morning was standing there with a tray of food. This time she said she would pick up the tray in the morning when she delivered food again. Mary said this is better than I expected.

Mary asked Tiberious how he had met Jesus. Tiberious said I was one of the Centurians that lifted his cross. Tiberious said after Jesus was placed in the tomb Pilate was so worried that Jesus' disciples would steal Jesus' body that he had 4 men put a rock in front of the entrance and then placed a guard in front of the tomb 24 hours a day. On the 3rd day one person walked up to the tomb a pushed the rock away. Jesus walked out of the tomb, in a robe, and walked away. The Centurian knew that no one would believe his story so he deserted the legion.

Tiberious said I came to the mount of Olives and to Golgotha every day. I fully expected Jesus to return, eventually. The day that Jesus and the disciples finally returned I was waiting for him to ask his forgiveness for my part in his crucifixion. Jesus came to me and called me by name and asked me to do him a favor. Tiberious said the favor Jesus asked of me was to take care of you for the rest of your human life. I readily agreed to do anything he wanted me to do. Jesus outlined every thing he expected of me. Jesus informed me that he would guide me to our final destination. I never asked how he would do this. I just relied on the faith I had in Jesus. Mary asked do you know how he will do this? Tiberious said he will guide us every day.

The time passed sometimes slowly but at last they made it to the port just outside of Rome. Upon departing the ship Tiberious started seeking transportation into Rome. Their were enough people selling rides into Rome, it was just a matter of negotiating a price. Finally Tiberious negotiated a price for the 2 of them to ride a cart into Rome. After entering the city they were dropped of at a lodging. Tiberious knew this probably was the cart drivers connection and he would get a commision for delivering them.

Tiberious negoiated for 2 nights lodging with meals for the 2 of them. The price was 2 pieces of silver.

After entering the room Tiberious said I have to check our finances. This will let me know what kind of transportation we can afford from here. Tiberious poured the silver out onto the bed and started counting. The surprise was that there was still 40 pieces of silver in the bag. Tiberious looked, in amazement, and said I think we are being taken care of from above. Mary said I think Jesus is traveling with us. Tiberious said only a person, or God, of that caliber could do something like this. Tiberious said this will give us enough money to purchase a form of transportation to get to where we are going. Tiberious said I have no idea of the final destination. Mary said I know where we are going but I don't know how to get there. Tiberious said have no fear we will be led to our destination.

Mary told Tiberious she would like to see Rome. I'm not sure that is a good idea, Tiberious said. Mary said I will cover up like I did on the ship. Tiberious said Rome is not the ship and you may not like what you see. Mary said maybe not, but I have never seen a big city before. Tiberious finally agreed but he said I need to see if I can make arrangements for our trip first. Mary said I will rest until you get back.

Tiberious approached the desk clerk and told him what he was looking for. The desk clerk asked how much money Tiberious wanted to spend. Tiberious was reluctant to give an amount but he realized that he had no choice in the matter. Tiberious asked if he could get a small cart and an animal to pull it? The clerk said I think I know of a place and I will let them know what you are looking for. Tiberious said this won't be a rental as I won't be bringing them back. The clerk said I will get you a good price. Tiberious said I need food for the animal and me in the cart and the cart set up so I can find a place to sleep. The clerk said all of that will be no problem. The clerk asked if Tiberious needed anything else? Tiberious said my companion wants to see the city. Tiberious asked if there was any place they should avoid? The clerk said they are building a new coleseum downtown, you may want to avoid the area. Tiberious said thank you and went back to their room.

Tiberious told Mary that his transactions had been made for their departure in 2 days so tomorrow they would be able to see Rome. Mary said I am hungry. Tiberious said there is a ristorante here that we can go and get something to eat. Mary asked if he knew any of the local dishes? Tiberious said Rome is known for their pasta so that would be a good start. Tiberious said you might want to be careful on what you order because the items may not be kosher. Mary said I am out of Judea now so I have to get used to the food and most of it won't be kosher. Tiberious allowed himself a small smile in recognition that Mary realized that her life would be very different from here on out.

The night, in the room, was uneventful. Tiberious again slept on the floor in front of the door. The room had no window so that was the only entry point to protect.

Tiberious' inner clock told him it was approaching the morning hour. Tiberious allowed himself to roll over and look under the door for a glimpse of daylight. As Tiberious turned back to the room he could see that Mary was up and sitting on the end of the bed. Mary said I think the kid wants some food. Tiberious asked how do you know if there might be more than one? Mary said a Mother just knows these things. Tiberious said I think we will be okay going to the ristorante this morning.

Mary reveled at the many fresh fruits that were available. Mary said I think Romans are spoiled. Tiberious answered they are privileged. Mary ordered the plate of fresh fruits plus dried meats. Tiberious asked Mary how she planned on eating every thing she ordered? Mary answered What I can't eat now I will save for later. Tiberious said I think it will get too warm and the fruit will spoil. Mary said then you will have to help me eat every thing on the plate. Tiberious allowed himself a smile. Guarding Mary Magdalene was turning into a labor of love for Tiberious.

Mary and Tiberious exited their lodging and headed for central Rome. Mary gushed over the paved streets and side walks. Mary said after the dusty roads of Judea this is paradise.

As they walked into the city Mary marveled at the fountains of running water. Tiberious explained that Rome had built a series of aquaducts to bring fresh water from the mountains to Rome. This series of aquaducts allowed for people to cook, drink and to bathe. Also this allowed for a way for the waste that people created daily to be taken away in the water. Mary asked where does the waste water go? Tiberious said it is used to irrigate the fields.

The day was spent walking and looking at all of the sites. Without notice Mary would duck into a shop. This sent Tiberious into a scurry to catch up to her. Every time he would admonish Mary for not telling him in advance but she still kept to what she was doing. Tiberious understood that Mary didn't realize how dangerous Rome could be.

As they stood outside of a curio shop a line of slaves, tied together in a tether, were paraded by. Mary asked Tiberious where they were being taken? Tiberious answered their is a slave market down town. Tiberious said if they are lucky they will be bought into a home or farm. Mary asked what happened to the ones who are not lucky? Tiberious answered some of them will be sent to the arena and trained as gladiators or used for sport. Mary asked what do you mean by sport? This was a delicate question for Tiberious to answer. Finally he said that they would be thrown into the arena with no formal training and with a modest weapon to be chased by a gladiator and killed. Mary asked what if the gladiator was killed instead? Tiberious pondered the question before answering that he didn't know because he had not seen this happen. Mary asked if he had ever been in the arena? Tiberious answered that he was trained as a soldier and had never been into an arena either as a participant or spectator. Mary was satisfied with Tiberious' answer and said that she was getting tired and it was time for them to head back to their lodging. Tiberious looked at the sky and realized that it was getting close to dusk and time for them to be off the street.

They had almost made it back to their lodging when a man approached them and with a knife drawn demanded their money. Tiberious said we have no money to give you. The man plunged at Tiberious with the knife and Tiberious and the man went to the ground with Tiberious holding the man in a wrestling move. The man soon realized he had picked on the wrong man as all of the training Tiberious had kicked in as they wrestled to the ground. Soon Tiberious stood up and the man was laying on the ground with his own knife plunged deeply into his chest. Tiberious told Mary they needed to hurry and get away from this area. Tiberious said we will be looked at differently because we are strangers in this city. Mary looked at Tiberious and noticed the blood on his tunic. Mary asked if Tiberious was hurt? Tiberious responded that the blood was the other man's blood. Mary saw that Tiberious' tunic was torn but she made the decision to wait until they got back to their room before asking more questions.

As soon as they entered their room Mary pulled up the tunic Tiberious was wearing and looked at his stomach. All Mary saw was a red mark, but no cut to the skin. Tiberious said I told you I was alright. Mary asked That Tiberious please be more careful in the future. This elicited a smile from Tiberious and a comment that he would do what he had to too protect them. Tiberious said we need to go to the ristorante and have something to eat. Tiberious said tomorrow will be here before you know it and we will be on the road. Tiberious was changing the subject and Mary knew that but she still responded with the last words, please be careful.

Tiberious was up before dawn and fidgeting to be on their way out of Rome. Mary finally got tired of watching Tiberious, with mostly closed eyes, and finally got up. Breakfast first, said Tiberious, and then we can get out of the room and be on our way.

As they went by the front desk the clerk said I have your cart out behind the building. Tiberious told Mary to go and order breakfast and he would join her after he inspected the cart.

Tiberious walked around the cart inspecting it for any damage that might not be apparent to most people. A donkey was hitched to a small cart with large wheels. The seat was just large enough for 2 people and the cart was filled with hay and under the seat was enough dried meats for a long trip. Some fresh fruit was included with 2 jugs of water. Tiberious said you did a good job of setting this up. The clerk said I had help. A stranger, to Rome, was there to help setting up the cart and too make sure it would be good enough for a trip. Tiberious handed the clerk the agreed upon funds for the cart and provisions. Tiberious didn't bother to ask how the funds would be split.

Tiberious joined Mary in the ristorante for breakfast. Mary had ordered a plate of fresh fruit and dried figs. Tiberious sat down accross from Mary and said we are ready to go. Mary said I took the opportunity to order breakfast for both of us. Tiberious looked at the meal and was impressed with Mary and said so.

Tiberious checked them out of the room and took Mary to the back of the lodging. Mary checked out their ride and was glad she had left all of this up to Tiberious. She would have had a problem making the right decisions.

Tiberious said he was told that a stranger had stepped forward to make sure everything was done right. Mary asked if Tiberious had asked about this man? Tiberious said I didn't think I had to. I believe everything we are doing is being guided. Mary agreed and said we need to be going.

The road North, out of Rome, was paved and an easy travel. Tiberious told Mary that Rome had taken the time to pave most of its roads. The roads were made of concrete and cobblestones close to Rome. Further away from Rome they were mostly hard sand and clay. The roads primary use was to move the military. This allowed Rome to move the military where it was needed fast and efficiently. The road close to Rome was jarring on the cart and made the ride uncomfortable. After about 10 kilometers the road turned to sand and clay. This would be easier on them and the donkey.

About 20 kilometers North of Rome the came upon a small creek. Tiberious could see that this had become a stop for most travelers and he pulled the cart over to the clearing next to the creek. Tiberious helped Mary out of the cart and then unleashed the donkey and led him to the creek. Tiberious held on to the donkey to make sure the donkey didn't drink too much and get bloated. Mary wandered a little down stream and then waded into the water. This made Tiberious a little nervous as he was holding the reins to the donkey and would have a hard time getting to Mary if she slipped. Just as Tiberious was going to say something to Mary she came out of the water and walked back to him. Mary said that felt good on my feet but the water is a little to cold to stand in for very long. Mary walked to a tree and sat down. Mary asked Tiberious to fetch some of the food. Mary said this is a good place for a lunch stop. Tiberious did as he was told with a little anxiety at the time being wasted.

Tiberious was relieved when they were back on the road. They would make it to Pisae before dark and that is where Tiberious planned to stop for the night. Roads, outside of Rome, were not safe to be on after dark.

Pisae was a little fiefdom small in size and ruled by a local landlord. Tibrious was told that the only lodging was controlled by this landlord and he would be over-charged. Tiberious asked if he had any other choices? The answer was chilling in scope by telling Tiberious everyone was afraid to go against this landlord. The landlord had a small army that he controlled. Tiberious asked where is the Roman who is supposedly in charge? Tiberious was told that the landlord had killed Rome's envoy and Rome hadn't replaced him because the land-lord had been careful to send the correct taxes to Rome.

Tiberious looked towards the mansion, that the landlord lived in, and could see how the landlord had exploited the people. As Tiberious gazed at the mansion a fire broke out. Within seconds the mansion was engulfed in flames and was totally gone within minutes. The villagers stepped back from Tiberious in fear and awe. Tiberious said I had nothing to do with the fire, I just happened to arrive when justice was dealt. A villager said Maybe you didn't set the fire but Justice was done as you entered our village. Tiberious became aware of the set up. Now the decision to spend the night or move on. It would be risky travling at night so Tiberious asked if there was a stable where he could board the donkey? A villager came foreword to offer a stable and Tiberious accepted.

Tiberious settled into the stable and told Mary that he would stay with the donkey and their cart. Mary said I am going to stay with you. Tiberious said I think they can find a bed for you. Mary said where you stay is where I stay. Tiberious didn't argue the point and set up a bed in the cart for Mary. Tiberious wasn't going to sleep all night.

Tiberious woke Mary long before dawn telling her we need to be on the road before daylight. Tiberious said we need to be far away from this village before they get up and find out we are gone. Mary wrapped a robe around herself and said I am ready.

Tiberious worked quietly out of the village and onto the road. They should be well on their way to Genua by sunrise.

Sunrise came and as it started to warm up Tiberious started to doze off. Mary asked if he had gotten any sleep? Tiberious said I stayed awake because I didn't know what was going to happen. Mary told Tiberious to get in the cart and get some rest. Mary said I can handle the donkey. Tiberious didn't argue the point and crawled back into the cart.

To Mary it seemed like even the donkey was in a hurry to leave Pisae behind. They moved up the road at a good speed. The only people they met, on the road, was a few peasants going to work in the fields. Most of them greeted them with a wave and a smile. None seemed curious as to why they were on the road. The woman, mostly veiled, didn't acknowledge anyone.

Tiberious finally stirred awake around noon and Mary pulled the cart into a large area of grass and trees that looked like it had been used for a rest area. Mary said I need to stretch my legs and find a place beyond the trees. Tiberious surpressed a smile but knew what was going to happen. After Mary came back to the cart Tiberious went behind the trees to relieve himself also. Mary had got some of the fruit and dried meat out for a lunch. Mary said I think the fruit won't last much longer. Tiberious said maybe we can shop for more in the next town. Mary asked Tiberious if he knew how far it was to Genua? Tiberious said it has beem a long time since I traveled this road but I think we should be there by dark. Tiberious said Genua is larger than Pisae and we should have no problem finding lodging.

True to his prediction they arrived at Genua before the sun went down. Lodging was easy to find and they found a place for the donkey and cart. After checking into their room Mary said I am hungrey for some hot cooked food. Tiberious laughed and said I can understand that. Luck was with them and a ristorante was just around the corner. Mary asked Tiberious if they dared to do some shopping here?

Tiberious said I think we are okay here. We just have to keep an eye out for pickpockets.

Mary was more cheerful than ever which was good, but it made Tiberious wonder what was in her mind. Tiberious had become very fond of Mary but he knew that their relationship would always be platonic.

After they had something to eat Mary and Tiberious went to an open market. Mary picked some fruit from the bins that she thought would last for awhile. Most of the fruit Mary was familar with as they were being grown in Palistine. The ones she didn't know she ignored. Tiberious paid for the fruit and they went back to their room. After they had settled in for the night Tiberious made a bed in front of the door. This was no time to take chances.

Tiberious was up before dawn and again woke Mary so she could do what women do in preparation for the day.

Luck was on their side and they found an open small ristorante to get something hot to eat. Tiberious asked Mary if she would be able to keep to a kosher diet? Mary said now that I am out in the world that is the least of my concerns. Mary said I am going to have to learn to eat what the locals eat. Tiberious said that is a good thing. You will not draw attention to yourself that way.

After picking up the donkey and cart, and Tiberious making sure the donkey had been fed and watered, they headed out on the road to Massila. Tiberious said we will be following along the sea on this part of the trip. Tiberious was worried that being this far from Rome they might be attacked by thieves.

The road that Rome had built was still in decent shape and they made good time. Tiberious stopped for lunch beside a small stream where they could rest. Tiberious scouted the area to make sure it was safe and then told Mary she could go to some trees and take care of anything she needed to do. Mary had learned to never question the wisdom that Tiberious was showing.

After a small respite they were back on the road. The donkey was picking up the pace, on his own. Tiberious said I don't think we can get to Massila before dark. He said I don't want to spend the night out on the road so I think we will keep moving. They actually did not meet any other travelers on the road, which Tiberious said was very strange.

They arrived in Massila after the moon had risen late in the evening. Tiberious spotted a stable on the edge of town. The stable was not locked and Tiberious entered with trepidation. As luck would have it a stablehand was sleeping just inside the door. After exchanging words, in a language Mary didn't understand, they were allowed to disconnect the cart and stable the donkey. Tiberious told Mary that they could sleep in the cart for the night. Tiberious told Mary they were in Gallia which was where he was born and raised.

The morning came and Tiberious didn't waste any time finding food and getting them back on the road. Tiberious explained that he didn't want to spend another late night on the road.

After they were back on the road Mary asked Tiberious how he had become a Roman centurian? Tiberious smiled as he explained the Roman generals had come to each village and enscripted all the young men into the legion. Tiberious explained that you weren't given any choice. Mary said that must have been horrible to be forced to leave home. Tiberious said it wasn't too bad. The legion was well fed and clothed. They even got a small stipend to spend any way they wanted. The hardest part was learning a new language every where I went. Tiberious said Palistine was the worse because the people didn't want them there. Mary said the soldiers were mean to the people. Tiberious said they were told the people were inferior and they could treat them any way they wanted, except they could not kill anyone without permission. Mary asked what happened if you crossed they line and killed someone? The centurian would be sent in to see the General and if they didn't have a good explanation they were executed. Mary said I never saw a centurian executed. Tiberious said this was always done where the people would not be able to see it.

This part of the trip, through the countryside, was an enjoyable experience. The people, on the road, were friendly and courteous. Tiberious explained that most of the people they were meeting were farmers and had led a life of detachment from the issues of politics.

They reached the small village of Logduinum early in the afternoon. Tiberious said we will spend the night here before we move on. Tiberious went directly to a stable to find lodging for the donkey and cart. This took them to the outscurts of the North side. After this Tiberious took Mary to the only place in town that had lodging. It was the right time of year because no one was traveling. Tiberious asked for, and got a room close to the front of the inn. The room included supper and breakfast.

Mary tried to ask where they could find a place to buy fresh fruit? Because the man couldn't understand Mary, Tiberious had to ask in the local language. The man answered Tiberious and they both had a laugh. Mary asked what were you laughing about? Tiberious said I explained that you were accompanying me and never had been in this country. Tiberious said I also said you were trying to fit in with the people we were visiting. This satisfied Mary and they left the inn to try to find some kind of fresh fruit.

The type of fruit was limited but the owner said for a price they could get some fruit that had come from an area closer to the sea. Tiberious said let me see what you have to offer.The owner led them to the back of shop and into a smaller room. All this time Tiberious kept Mary behind him and his hand close to the knife

he always carried. After entering the room, and see-
ing no one else Tiberious relaxed some. In the room they found several kinds of melons and some fruit that Tiberious had never seen before. Tiberious told Mary to pick out what she wanted and he would pay for it.

After they were back in the room Mary asked if the fruit was very expensive? Tiberious said the man was more honest than he figured he would be and that he didn't even try to negotiate a cheaper price. Tiberious said we have to be careful. Most people don't have the cash money to buy imported fruit. Tiberious said I always worry that the news well get out about us having cash money. This could set us up to be robbed. Mary said I have you to protect us.

Again Tiberious slept on the floor with his back on the door. A very uneventful but restless night. Tiberious was up just before dawn. This amazed Mary at how he could tell it was time to get up. Tiberious led Mary out to the courtyard where she could relieve herself and wash up. Tiberious did the same and then led Mary into the dining area. 2 guests were already at the table and being served. The breakfast consisted of differnt types of bread, local churned butter and jams.

When they were through eating Mary asked Tiberious to ask their host if they could buy some of the bread? The host let them buy 2 loaves of bread and explained that he had no way to package the butter and jam.

Back on the road again Mary asked Tiberious if he ever wanted to go back home? Tiberious answered that he had left that life long ago and he had no desire to ever go back. Tiberious said farm work was a dawn to dark job with no time off for relaxing. Tiberious said being a centurian meant long days of training but there was always time off and you got to travel to interesting places, even though Palistine wasn't a choice duty station. In Palistine the people hated the Romans and you always had to be on the alert for dangerous people. Mary said I think, mostly, both sides hated each other equally. Tiberious said you are probably right on that.

The people they met on this part of the trip were mostly farmers and were friendly with a wave and a smile. Tiberious greeted the people in their native language which made this part of the trip more enjoyable. Mary said the people are friendly to strangers. Tiberious said my understanding of the language makes us as locals and not strangers.

They entered Lutetia before dark and Tiberious went directly to a stable. Tiberious explained to Mary this is the town he grew up in. Mary asked if his parents were still living here? Tiberious said I don't know but I have no desire to find out. Mary didn't push the issue knowing that Tiberious would only answer what he wanted to.

Lutetia was large enough to have a choice of lodging and Tiberious took them to an inn close to the river. Tiberious explained to Mary that being close to the river meant that the lodging should be cleaner as this is where most travelers stayed. Mary asked Tiberious if there was a local religion? Tiberious said that Rome had banned all local religions to establish only those religions worshipped by Rome. Mary asked Tiberious where he had grown up? Tiberious said his family had a small farm outside of town. Mary asked if they would be going by the farm? Tiberious said I have no desire to go by the farm. Mary asked don't you want to see your parents? Tiberious said my Mother is dead and I didn't get along with my Father. Mary asked if he had any siblings? Tiberious said I have 2 brothers and I think they are still living on the farm. Tiberious said I was glad to get away from the farm that is why I didn't resist when Rome came calling. Mary said I am hungry let's go find some food.

Morning came to early for Mary. She told Tiberious that she hoped they would get to where they are going soon. Mary was getting tired of traveling and it showed on her face. Tiberious said we can spend another day here for you to rest. Tiberious added I don't know how far we have to go. Mary asked if he would know when he got to where they were going? Tiberious said I think it will be made obvious to us.

Mary spent most of the day in bed. It was in the late afternoon when she finally told Tiberious that she had to go do her thing and would like to see a little of the town. Tiberious agreed and said we will stay close to the inn, but we will be able to see a lot of the town.

As Mary and Tiberious walked along the river Mary was intrigued with the architecture of the buildings and asked Tiberious if the Romans had influenced the buildings. Tiberious said most of these buildings were here before the Romans. Tiberious said the rich had built their homes close to the river to be close to the water. Tiberious said this was dangerous because the poor people who lived upstream also used the river as a bathroom. Mary laughed and said you are telling me to not drink the water. Tiberious said if you drink the water it will probably go through you fast and you will lose some weight. Mary said okay point taken. Sometimes Tiberious' sense of humor came out.

The morning dawned bright and clear. Tiberious said we should be able to make it to Gesoriacum early and find passage accross to Britannia. Mary asked if that would be their final destination? Tiberious stated I really don't know. You will have to ask the donkey, he is the one who has been leading us. Mary just chuckled because she knew Tiberious was only partially serious. They had been following the donkey as if it was a human.

Following the river they met farmers on their way to the fields or to market. To Mary it seemed that all of them were friendly. Tiberious said this far from Rome they don't have any fear.

They entered Gesoriacum early in the afternoon. This gave Tiberious enough time to find passage for them and the donkey. The hard part was the donkey and cart. It seems no one wanted to take an animal and cart accross the water. Finally Tiberious was able to secure passage, at an extreme cost. The boat Captain told Tiberious to be at the dock before the sun came up. The Captain also told Tiberious if the water was rough the trip would be postponed or even cancelled. This water was very unpredictable. Tiberious said that he understood. Tiberious assured himself that the water would be calm tomorrow. It was just that feeling that came over you when everything was right.

Tiberious told Mary that tonight they would make sure the donkey was well taken care of. Also it was time to shop for fruit to take with them for the crossing. Mary said we also need to find some heavy wraps because it probably will be cold on the water. With a nod from Tiberious they set off in search of the items they would need.

The next morning they approached the dock and the boat they would be taking. The boat was really just an old scow with an open deck. The donkey didn't even hesitate as it was loaded on the boat. A good omen to Tiberious. Tiberious secured the cart and then found a sheltered place for Mary to sit out of the wind. The crossing would take most of the morning, if they were lucky.

They docked in Londincum before noon and Tiberious made the descision to push on. Something in the back of his head told him not to stay here.

Late afternoon they entered the village of Roslyn. As soon as they entered Mary said Jesus and I were here. Tiberious understood that this is where they were supposed to be.

A woman came up to Mary and said welcome home. This time the language was clear to Mary. Tiberious asked if there was a place he could stable the donkey? Tiberious was directed to a local farmer who had goats and was willing to take the donkey on his farm. Mary was directed to an empty house. Mary was told this house was left for her to use as long as she needed.

Tiberious came back into the village and was greeted by one of the Elders. The Elder asked Tiberious if he was here to finish the church Jesus had asked them to build? Tiberious said I am here to help any way I can. The Elder led Tiberious to where the church had been started. The Elder explained that Jesus had laid out size of the church. He explained they had used the ingenuity the Romans had used on the roads to build the foundation and floor. The Elder explained that they were having trouble with the walls. Tiberious smiled and said I think I know the magic potion we will need to use. Tiberious went to the road and dug up some material on the edge of the road. Tiberious asked if they knew where the Romans had found the black dirt? A young man smiled and said I can show you where it came from.

When they entered the pit from where the black dirt came from Tiberious recognized that it was black ash. Tiberious said this is exactly what we need. We can mix this with sand and lime and it will form a strong bond to keep the rocks in place for the walls. Again this was a job for the donkey and the cart.

Everything was becoming clear to Tiberious. He was here not only to take care of Mary but to finish the church. Jesus, always a mystery, had made himself clear.

Tiberious had been working on the church for several months when one of the children came running over and told him to come quick Mary was going to have her baby. Tiberious set off on a dead run and when he got to the house a midwife was already there. Mary was being tended to and Tiberious was stopped at the door. He was told he wasn't needed inside the house. Tiberious walked around the house that seemed like an eternity. Finally a child's cry was heard from inside the house. The midwife came out and said you can go into the house now.

Tiberious entered the house and Mary was cradling a baby. Mary said this my Daughter, Maria St. Magi. Tiberious said she is beautiful. Her Father would be proud.

The church built at Roslyn was exceptionally strong so it would stand the test of time. The elders had taken it amongst themselves to appoint 2 priests to oversee the functions of the church. These priests were to see that all information would be kept private and passed down through the ages. The secrets that Tiberious had relayed to them would be kept secret in the church and only told to the ones who needed to know.

The priests, in turn, would appoint their successors. This way all the important information would be protected.

Maria had just turned 6 years old when Mary got sick. At night Tiberious would lay awake as Mary would talk to Jesus. Tiberious would go to the church every day and ask if Jesus would heal Mary. Tiberious never got an answer.

Finally a day after Mary got weaker she told Tiberious that a woman in the village would be tasked with raising Maria. Mary said Jesus has told me you must be free of the responsibility. Tiberious protested that he didn't mind the responsibility. Mary said Jesus had told her that you wouldn't be allowed to stay in the village that long. Tiberious understood but he said he could take Maria with him. Mary said Maria needs to be here to keep the secret. Mary said my time, on this earth, is up. Jesus has told me my soul can go live with him but my human body must stay behind.

That night Tiberious was more alert than before. He knew that the end was near for Mary and he could do nothing to stop it. Early after the sun went down and the evening chill was in the air Tiberious saw Mary's breath float out of her body and rise in the air and dis-appear. Tiberious waited awhile before he stepped out the door. To Tiberious' surprise most of the village had gathered around the door. Tiberious told a priest that it was over. Mary had gone to be with Jesus.

The midwife and another lady entered the house with clean rags, water and a robe. They took their time to do a thorough job of cleaning Mary and then dressing her in a white robe. The 2 priest, with 4 young men were summoned to the house. They brought a special casket that they had built. The casket was carved out of a large tree and cut diagonally in half. Gently they place Mary in the casket and carried her to the church. Mary was placed on a diaz and the top of the casket was removed for everybody to pay their respects.

Mary was kept in state for only 24 hours and then the top of the casket was put in place. The top was seal-ed with sap from a pine tree.

The top of the casket had been intricatley carved to show a woman in repose in a robe, bare feet showing, arms folded across her breast and a scarf over her head. The carving was beautiful and must have been planned for a long time. The 2 priest and 4 young men picked up the casket and carried it to the back of the church. They carried the casket down some steps and under the church. There in the dirt area an alcove had been carved out just large enough for the casket to fit. After the casket was placed in the alcove the area was sealed with dirt, lime and ash. It was done so well that no trace of the placement of the casket remained.

Tiberious waited the 3 days of mourning, by Roman standards, and then informed the elders he was leaving. He assured them he would return every so often to check on things here.

Tiberious said good bye to Maria, letting her know she was in good hands. Maria smiled at Tiberious and then ran off to play.

Tiberious stopped at the edge of the village and looked back at what he was leaving. Tiberious smiled to himself remembering the words Jesus had uttered on the cross. "Thou shalt tarry until I return". Now he understood that Jesus meant he would be the one to carry the secret forward. Tiberious' job in future generations would be to make sure every descendant knew where they had come from and to teach them how to keep the secret. Because he would not age over time, Tiberious wouldn't be allowed to stay long any where.

EPILOGE

This story is based in European Mythology and Native Folklore. It is not meant to be fact based even though I have taken pains to make sure most of the spelling of cities, towns, villages and some countries are correct for the time period. I have left the names of some areas blank, with only a description to tantalize the reader. I did not intentionally disrespect any religion in writing this novel.